DWIGHT'S FLIGHT

BY KIM THOMPSON

ILLUSTRATED BY BRETT CURZON

A Little Honey Book

Crabtree Publishing
crabtreebooks.com

Introduction

This decodable story supports children as they:

1. Learn to read the high-frequency words shown below.

2. Learn to discriminate between the **short i** sound heard in *sit* and the **long i** sound heard in *sight*.

3. Learn to read words in which the **long i** sound has the spelling pattern **igh**.

Use the resources here to review sounds, letters, and words with young readers. Then, help them find and read the **long i** words in the story. Find more learning resources beginning on page 22. Happy reading!

High-Frequency Words

a	down	says
again	eats	sees
all	fly	so
at	he	soon
be	like	up
blue	not	what
cannot	red	yellow

Sounds and Letters

The letters **i**, **g**, and **h** form a vowel team. The **igh** team makes the **long i** sound. It sounds like the letter **i** saying its name.

Look at these words. The word *sit* has the **short i** sound you know. The word *sight* has the **long i** sound.

sit

sight

Read. Make the **long i** sound when you see **igh**.

night

right

fright

flight

3

Dwight eats.

Dwight eats.

4

He eats all night.

It will soon be light.

Wind spins in.

It spins with might!

Dwight spins down.

Dwight is in flight!

"Not this!" says Dwight.

"What a fright!

This is up high!

This is NOT all right!"

Dwight grips.

Dwight grips tight.

He will be so still.

It might be all right.

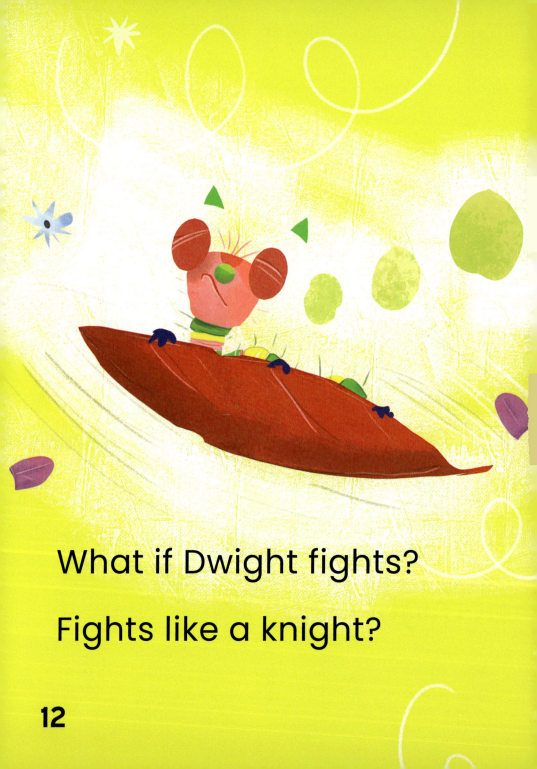

What if Dwight fights?

Fights like a knight?

This plight might be up.

It might be all right.

Dwight cannot fight.

Not at this height.

So Dwight sits up.

He sees big sights!

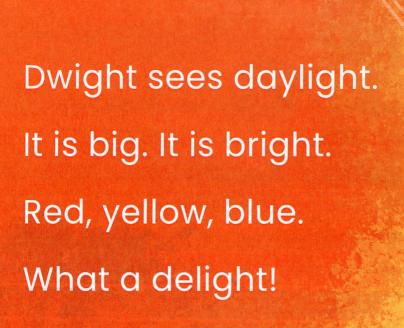

Dwight sees daylight.

It is big. It is bright.

Red, yellow, blue.

What a delight!

A slight hit.

Down sinks Dwight.

"What a flight!" he says.

Dwight is all right!

Dwight sighs.

He LIKES flight.

Will Dwight fly again?

He might!

I Can Read!

Read **short i** words from the story.

big	in	sits	will
grips	is	spins	wind
hit	it	still	with
if	sinks	this	

Read **long i** words from the story.

bright	height	right
daylight	high	sighs
delight	knight	sights
Dwight	light	slight
fights	might	tight
flight	night	
fright	plight	

Read sentences with **long i** words.

A red knight fights.

It spins right in flight.

This night-light is bright.

I Can Write!

Write each word on a piece of paper. Add **igh** in the blank. What word did you make? Use the words to write sentences or stories.

I Can Think!

1. What helps Dwight not be afraid?

2. Do you think Dwight will fly someday? Why?

3. Read the secret words. Find their pictures in the story.

highway   **twilight**   **upright**

DWIGHT'S FLIGHT

Written by: Kim Thompson
Illustrated by: Brett Curzon
Designed by: Rhea Magaro
Series Development: James Earley
Educational Consultant: Marie Lemke M.Ed.

Crabtree Publishing

crabtreebooks.com   800-387-7650

Copyright © 2024 Crabtree Publishing

All rights reserved. No part of this publication may be reproduced, stored in a retrieval system or be transmitted in any form or by any means, electronic, mechanical, photocopying, recording, or otherwise, without the prior written permission of Crabtree Publishing.

Printed in the U.S.A.
112023/PP20230920

Published in Canada
Crabtree Publishing
616 Welland Ave.
St. Catharines, Ontario
L2M 5V6

Published in the United States
Crabtree Publishing
347 Fifth Ave
Suite 1402-145
New York, NY 10016

Library and Archives Canada Cataloguing in Publication
Available at Library and Archives Canada

Library of Congress Cataloging-in-Publication Data
Available at the Library of Congress

Hardcover: 978-1-0398-3583-2
Paperback: 978-1-0398-1826-2
Ebook (pdf): 978-1-0398-3593-1
Epub: 978-1-0398-3603-7
Read-Along: 978-1-0398-3613-6
Audio: 978-1-0398-3623-5